Bend. Human Willing.

sean::adrian::brijbasi

Published simultaneously in the United States
and Great Britain in 2023
by Pretend Genius
Copyright © Sean::Adrian::Brijbasi

ISBN: 979-8-9859089-6-1

other books by Sean::Adrian::Brijbasi

One Note Symphonies
for Emma

Still Life in Motion
for those who play
Marius and Andréus

The Unknowed Things
for Julius

The Dictionary of Coincidences, Volume i
for Emma

S{E}AN?
for EM{M}A+

E{M}MA+ the ghost orchids
for Emma

darling two hearts
for E{M}MA+ the ghost orchids

Stories for Nadira
for Adrian, Andréus, Elijah, Helena, Julius,
Marius, Nadira

Play Championship World-Class
Tennis with Bjorn McEnroe
*for Adrian, Andréus, Elijah, Helena, Julius,
Marius, Nadira*

The World That Destroyed the World
*for Adrian, Andréus, Elijah, Helena, Julius,
Marius, Nadira*

The Book of Lashonda
*for Adrian, Andréus, Elijah, Helena, Julius,
Marius, Nadira*

ENTROPALACE
for my brother Troy

NO ONE CAN SEE THE WORLD I LIVE IN
for the only one

M.A.R.I.A.201001000
for my sister Simone

for

Emma

"Es ist immer etwas Wahnsinn in der Liebe. Es ist aber immer auch etwas Vernunft im Wahnsinn."

— FN

Table of. Contents.

So turn on. 35
And in the morning. 36
At night. 37
At the playground. 38
If she. 39
Some people. 40
We'll climb. 41
Some days. 42
During the collapse. 43
And see. 44
You're hiding. 45
It's not. 46
And I'll stand. 47
And above. 48
I'll pretend. 49
And dream. 50
I don't know. 51
We're strangers too. 52
But there. 53
I remember. 54
On a day 55
Like we did. 56
In school. 57
Or in. 58
And not losing. 59
I see. 60
I would see. 61
The next day. 62
Another letter. 63
The trees. 64
You'll hear. 65
But I didn't. 66
We can leave. 67
Then at night. 68
Something magical. 69

foreword by the author

ignore all punctuation dont stop

the tree is too tall. ~~this !!~~
~~Tree is too tall.~~ Practice
piano on the table. light
coming through the school-
window. an examination
- of the tree itself. the ?
(trees know, or archilochus
(colubris? days of Rain.
nights of ~~Dreams~~. pretending
~~(not) to hear the music~~.

Before umbrellas. When it rained. People waited. Under trees. They waved. And sometimes called. To each other. Across the way. We were caught. In such a time. Small animals. Ran by. The wind. Bent the flowers. Towards me. And then. Towards you. Birds flew. Across the sky. Above us. For me. They disappeared. Behind the tree. For you. They travelled. Over. Until they became. Specks of dust.

It was of understanding. Such things. From the past. To be caught. When someone. Could not know. The sky. But to be. Caught. As we are. Today. Can be. Of meaning. Because the sky. Can be known. And so. It might. Be of meaning. If I were caught. In the rain. And if you. Were caught. In the rain. And we waited. Under a tree. Forgetting. Remembering. Or of a separate. And singular. Despair.

I should think. Instead about. How beautiful. You are. And you should think. Instead. About how beautiful. I am. And while thinking. Feel. The air. Around us. After the rain. Stops. Of a familiar. And sweet. Feeling. Though of a different. Sweetness. But I can think. Only about death. And you can. Think only. About death. We people. Who wait. Under trees. After the invention. Of umbrellas.

It's like we don't live. In the world. History happens. Around us. The different layers of history. Above us. And history written. Without us. But nothing of. Your sleeping positions. And nothing of. My sleeping positions. We can ask. Each other. When we meet. Describe. The human formations. Before you lie. Awake. And before I lie. Awake. And see. What only few. See. Though won't. Or can. But vaguely remember.

And your favourite book. Somewhere in the blanket. Between us. A history of the trees. Used before. (The invention of) umbrellas. The paths followed. From all around. Drawings of how they. Might have looked. And where. They might be. Found some sketched. With the animals. That ran past them. Or the birds. That took their rest. Upon them. Or how. They appeared. Under the sun. When they were. Also used. But not. For waiting.

I watch your eyes. Closed during sleep. You lying. On the bed. Your eyelashes. Like wild flowers. Growing on your. Eyelids. Your hair. Flowing. From your head. And the darkness. In this room. The dark sky. Behind them. The tenderness in. Your face. And your skin. Has its own breath. I wonder. Where you are now. As the breeze moves. Through the open window. I feel it. And see it wake. Your skin. Like how it wakes the grass. Outside. My perfect person. Who waited. Under a tree (how lucky for me). And becoming more. Perfect. Everyday.

We can return. To this place. And watch the grass. Along the hill. Surmise the wind. Moving over it. And the grass itself. Moving. Like people. Though standing still. But the people. Not like grass. Instead like wood. Each person. A piece of kindling. For the great. And ever burning fire. Of sorrow. Fascinating those. Who aren't yet. In it. And who think. Having never. Been burned. It does good. And it still. Might do. Who can say? Because everyone catches. Fire. Some day.

Together or alone. We can return. To this place. To this night. To this close night. Together or alone. To this dark night. Folding. Over us. Our shoulders here. Our faces here. Our arms and hands. Here. Our eyes and lips. Here. But our legs. As if they belong. Somewhere else. Already moving. Towards day. And the light. We need to live. But that interferes. With how close. We get. To feeling an understanding. Of something.

Maybe the one thing. The one. Atom of a thing. In this night. And if not this night. Then another. That splits. And splits again. The one thing. That splits. And splits again. Until you and I. In our minds. Spread. Across the world. Across time. We who travel. By night. By the carriage. Of night. Always waiting. Its door open. And inside. Two seats ready. For us to start. Again. Though sometimes we go. Without each other. Or not at all.

But the day. Can take us too. Beneath the summer. Trees. Sunlight passing through. Gently swaying. Leaves. And the breeze. That makes us pause. In the middle of it. All comes. From the night. It travels. Everywhere. Together. They took us. Here. As it rained. You waited. And me. Neither thinking. Of the sky. And the wind. Someone stopped. And spoke to you. With a black. Umbrella. You sent him. Away.

I would have stopped. Too. Even though. Someone I knew. Died that day. I remember. Seeing her sing. When I was young. But hadn't seen her. Since. She didn't know me. Though I thought of her. Once or twice. A year. Or every other. Because she was. There. And I was young. I couldn't remember. Her face. She had lifted. Her dress. To hide it. Not on purpose. Though it did. I saw your face. Then you (looking up). I saw your neck.

The rain falling. Just outside. Your space. If I were closer. I would have seen. A drop. Or two. Touch your skin. I heard people. Talking in line. That's how I knew. They were sad. And liked her. More than me. But I felt. A small sadness too. It would have. Been nice. To know her. Better. But I. Only thought of her. Vaguely. She became famous. And lived. A good life. If we meet. I hope. You don't. Ask me questions. About her. I wouldn't be able. To piece it. Together.

It's like the past. In the distance. An open door. On the horizon. I returned by train. And saw it. As the sleeper. Passing by. Blurred. What little I could. Make out. Through that far-off. Aperture. But pulling in. And more awake. One could say. To the present. I saw the crane. Above the buildings. Swinging. Slowly clockwise. Its shadow ticking. Along the shops. And sun-bleached awnings. Of brasseries. And busy downtown. Streets. Where existence. Though imperilled. By machines. And the coming together. Of so many. People. Always seemed. To be. In reach.

And then a child. Riding. The family donkey. Pulled along the river. By her father. In the closeness. Of this night. Feathered crowns of large. And small. Birds. The brightly colored. Blankets. And women. Spinning. In brightly colored. Skirts. In the closeness. Of this night. The reflection. Of a candle. Lit. In the window. The glass revealing. A hidden light. That itself. Reveals. Nothing. And there. Just behind it. The shabby balcony. Never used. Though from outside. To someone passing by. Has the look. Of not a bad place. To be.

They can't see us. In here. You talking softly. Almost. Not talking. At all. About going there. One day. Was it you (as I touched your hair)? And your father. Together in the sun. You say. We will. Go together. One day. But until then. You'll wait. Under a tree. And I'll wait. Under a tree. No one knew. Not even one. Of so many. Billions. How happy I was. To see you. Send him. Away. How could anyone. With an umbrella. Understand. People like us.

xvi

But I knew you. Were there. Unlike other times. When I didn't. When someone passing. Behind me. Stopped. Because he. Or she. Saw your face. Above the line. Of my shoulder. A short distance. Away while. I looked. Elsewhere. Maybe you glanced. In this direction. Then a backfire. Birds scatter. As if the leaves. Disperse from. The branches. Above you disappearing. Into a grey. Sky that goes on. Forever. And is both. Everywhere. And nowhere. At once.

Then you. Standing. On a black square. Of your kitchen. Floor. Looking through. The kitchen window. As rain. Falls and collects. In puddles. On the concrete path. From your door. To uncertain destinations. The water boiling. In a small pot. On your kitchen stove. The steam. Settling as small. Drops. On the ceiling. Above. Two or three. So heavy. They fall. And outside. The sun. Light penetrates. The haze. You didn't think. Or didn't care. The rain. Would come again. So soon. Though all around. There were clouds.

We know. The same song. You could sing it. With me. If the backfire. Were part. Of a barrage. And I was hit. In a vital place. Or the other way. Around. Though I can't bear. To think of it. We can go through. The catalogue. In our heads. And find. A song. We both know. The words to. And sing together. Probably one. We learned as children. Something our mothers. Or fathers. Sang to us. Something. We can remember. And sing. Together. As it rained. Over us. Without umbrellas. My head. Or your head. In your lap. Or mine. Your sound. And my sound. Meeting. In the space. Between. And behind each. A small body. A small life. A small world.

It's like you're sad. In my living room. While outside. Rain falls. On the window. The day. Goes by. Like this. And when I speak. To piece. Together. Words that mean. Something. The less I see. Even those half-spoken. The letters. Grow in number. And size. In front of me. And block my view. In this small world. I have to find. The right balance. To speak. To you. Or see you. Whole. In silence. I have so much. To say. But you are. So beautiful. Framed by the window. And the rain. Behind it. That from in here. Cries out. For help. It's okay. If you cry too.

And the wind. Picking through the trees. Cleaning them. Of dying leaves. The runner. The walker. Tripping over. Something unseen. Tumbling. To the ground. Down there. Rough. And wet. Scraping. Human skin. Washed away. By randomly forming. Channels. Though traces. Still remain. We hold. Everything. In the smallest. Gesture. The smallest turning. Of our head. To the untrained. Eye looks. Like stillness. And the smallest lifting. Of our brow. That suggests intention. And is intention. Itself. We hold everything. In there.

And among so many. Channels. There is one. That starts straight. From you. Diverted here and there. By detritus. And then again. Straight through. Drops that fell. From the leaves. And landed. At your feet. The start. Of a path. An umbrella would. Have started. One. That didn't start. With you. I can see it. Shining clear. Lit up. On the darkened street. As clouds drift. Over us. And though losing. Sight of it. Somewhere in between. I know it's coming. My way. And with the smallest. Gesture. The smallest. Lifting of my brow. Will it through.

Some people. Are born. And add. Something meaningful. To the world. It's just. A coincidence. You lean over me. Turning the sky dark. I think. You have perfect ears. For dangling. Earrings. I was there. Lying. On the ground. You lifted me. By my legs. And wheeled me. Into the backyard. Shed. Like a wheel. Barrow. Where the light. Peeked through. A crease. And jealous. Of what happens. In the darkness. Cut through. The space. Between us. And then half. A coincidence. Bending itself. Around. My turning head. Shined. On the golden. Button stud. Someone had dropped. Right there.

xxiii

I see. A bird. It looks. Like it's watching us. First me. Then you. I could almost. Make out. Your shape. In its black eye. One of those. That didn't leave. When the others. Flew away. Brave bird. All the others. Will return. And make it seem. Like you. Had flown. Away too. But you stayed. To see the beginning. You could sing. The story. To them. If you thought it. Interesting. Of two people. Waiting. Under different trees. In the rain. Without umbrellas. Or maybe. You'll fly. Away. When the last one. Has returned.

We're not. The only ones. From up there. You'll see. Everything. As each drop. Of rain. Falls. Like a note. From a prelude. Rings. Softly on the grass. Within. The impression. Of our bodies. Where we once. Lay. Loudly on the letter. Box. That if our hands. Had ears. Would go deaf. As they reached. In there. But no one. Writes letters. Anymore. I'll write one. To you. Something. You can read. Out loud. When you're at home. But out loud. Softly. If someone. In another room. Lurking. Just to breathe. Might hear.

So dear you. An altogether faithful. Friend. Who has. Never seen. Me at the height. Of my power. I do. Reach it. Alone. Now and then. One day. You'll open a door. And behold. A great undertaking. My body. Standing above. The kitchen table. The potted. Lemon tree. A ball. Rolling. Underneath the spotted. Red and white. Settee. Think of these. As structures. Of a great. City and me. Like a great. Man moving. Among them. Careful not to do. The damage. Great men do. Because you. Will walk here. And breathe here.

What we do. Alone. Can be shown. But rarely seen. You will see. One day. We use all. Our powers. To be born. And are powerless. Soon after. But we can become. Powerful again. I'll part. The curtains. With enough space. For you. To peek in. Find your way. Between. The rows of trees. Walk. Nearer to the grass. And not in. The middle. Of the barren. Path. A promenade. Unobserved. In your solitude. An afternoon. Breeze. Cooling your legs. As you raise. Your dress. And wade. Through a shallow. Stream. I ask myself. Which I prefer. The certainty. Or uncertainty. Of your absence.

Then after crossing. Find a quiet place. To rest. And watch. The clouds drift. Slowly by. Before moving on. I'll think of you. There. Alone. And imagine. No one. Knows. The history. Of that moment. And if remembered. Remembered only. By you. I'll turn cards. During the interlude. The King. The Three. The Eight. The Queen. I'll wait. Until dark. Until. The next day. I'll wait. And if it rains. I'll know where. To find you. From your favorite. Book. I'll know. Under which tree. To look. Everything is. Out there. And you too. Sincerely. Or love. Or very truly. Yours.

We can't share. The terror. Around which. Our bodies. Are wrapped. We can't share. The terror. Of our brains. And everything. That's trapped. In there. We use sounds. But can't speak. Our minds. Words drift away. From our perfectly. Ordered sentences. Like sand. From small. And perfectly. Ordered mounds. Undone. With the slightest. Breath. And with them. Most of what. We mean. Though not all. Something remains. A microscopic amount. Like protoplasm. In a speck. Of dust. On a distant planet. Just enough. For us. To declare. Victoriously. That together. We have found. Life.

Perhaps when. You arrive. We'll embrace. Like scientists. Like people. Who observe. I observe you. Now. Under a tree. But in many years. I will remember. This time. Only in connection. With its end. As I remember. All things. And therefore. Sadness. I've heard said. Flowers die. So we can. Remember them. In winter. And the hem. Of your dress. Still wet. You'll tell me. How you crossed. In bare feet. Lifting it. And I'll remember. Instead. That I was there. Waiting for you. On the other. Side. Then taking off. My shoes and socks. Wade in. To meet you. Halfway. Though I never did. I hope our time. Together. Will be long.

But under. Your tree. You seem. Tired. And to you. Maybe I seem. Tired too. Our days. Filled. With too many. Things to do. To observe. Like scientists. And it may seem. Like nothing. Will be left. For us after. We've worn. Ourselves out. From waking. And walking. And talking. And waking. Again. And again. As machines. Incessantly hum. And feet. Incessantly drum. We'll be. Too exhausted. To fight. The weakest current. But in the end. Also too exhausted. To pretend. To say. Too many words. Or do. Too many things. And instead. Say. To each other. And do. For each other. Only what is. Essential.

xxxi

Give me. That and nothing. More. No extra. Thought. Or gesture. Or concern. Don't use. A single. Extra syllable. And speak. No louder than. A whisper. When I'm near. But even. From far away. Make it spare. With me. Hide yourself. To others. With long soliloquies. Clothed. In layers. Of the latest. Fashion. Show sympathy. And hold those. Who suffer. Some small. Despair. But don't. Hold me. We people. Who wait. Under trees. After the invention. Of umbrellas.

But of the distance. Now. The space. From this tree. To that. Which seems. Like nothing. To another. And maybe. In the end. Nothing. To us. I see you. In your summer. Dress. Your hair. Wet. A few strands. Unfastened. From your skin. Like arms. Reaching out. To the air. And with the lightest. Touch. Fastened again. It's enough. For you. To stand there. And be beautiful. I learned. To become beautiful. Maybe you. Learned too. Though it's hard. For me. To believe. You weren't born. A genius.

So turn on. All the lights. While I'm away. You don't. Have to search. The house. In secret. I should have. Turned them on. For you. To let you know. The photographs are there. To be picked up. And pondered. The sofa. To lie upon. The ceiling. To look up to. And wonder. As your body. Sinks. Into the cushions. But through the window. There is light. Coming from the moon. I know its phases. From the morning. Paper. Though I didn't think. I'd return. Breathless. To find you. Partly illuminated. Full. And that night. Unable to sleep. Because I couldn't stop. Thinking. About what I saw. And how beautiful. You really are.

And in the morning. I'll go. You'll wave. From another room. I'll think. About turning back. But I can't think. Like that. Every. Time. I see you. Watching me. From the window. Alone I love. The darkness. But with you. I love. The light too. And I can find. The darkness. In the light. Small spaces. And times. Moments. When you're distracted. To reach. The surface. From beneath. Your bright sea. Your sunlight steeped. World. Your living. Dream. To feel. The darkness. On my skin. To see. The darkness. And take it. All in. To breathe. My dark air. Before returning. To the light. And to you again.

At night. I cross. Flat roads. Turn corners. To more. And then the door. The stairs. Another door. Opened. To the surprise. Of you. I see the walls. On either side. The photographs. From a life. I don't yet. Know. Hung there. And start across. The flat floor. I'll spy them. In my periphery. Make out. Your face. In one or two. But someone stops. To talk. To you. She closes. Her umbrella. You smile. Or from here. It looks. To me so. I see your mouth. Moving. Though I can only. Hear the rain. On metal. On concrete. On elements. Of the earth. Like wood. And the leaves. Above me. I'll stay here. Until it ends. And maybe. A little after.

At the playground. The swing. And slide. Are wet. But underneath. A girl. Who stayed. Too long. When all. The other. Children left. Also waits. The noise. On the hard plastic. Shell. Hides the sound. Of thunder. Heard for miles. Around. Her mother. Comes. To walk. Her home. They'll hold hands. Beneath an umbrella. She keeps. By the front. Door. Next to. The little one. The girl forgets. Though it's not. There. For her to take. And the mother. Will be happy. But she'll be. Sad too.

xxxvii

If she. Only had. The likeness. Of your face. To touch. She would. Whether made. Of bronze. Or clay. She'll put. Her arms. Around you. One strand. Of hair. To hold. Not a head. Of hair. To brush. She'll collect. Broken. Pieces. From your stone. Hold them. Tight. So her hands. Cut up. And the blood. What's in it. Was. In you too. Was the start. Of you. Everything. Ends. Though if. She's wrong. You're still. Around. Somewhere. She can send. A message to. From time. To time. She thinks. Like this.

xxxviii

Some people. Know. This way. Of living. The woman said. Good-bye. And glanced. At me. As if. In secret. But I saw. And it was. As if. In secret. You glanced. At me too. She opened. Her umbrella. And in the distance. Above. The weathered. Dome. Starlings. Escaped. The oculus. And flew 'til. They were gone. She started. In that. Direction. My eyes. Followed her. Though not. For long. I could imagine. How she walked. After I saw. Her walk. To you.

xxxix

We'll climb. The stairs. There. The ones. She climbed. Days before. To sit. In the empty. Nave. And hear. The choir sing. Their sacred songs. Past. The couple. Talking. And the girl. Studying. Her lesson book. Who distracted. By our footsteps. Will pause. To take. A look. She's reading about. Organic chemistry. The different. Expressions. Of enthalpy. And from. Up there. She can see. The bus. And most. Of the path. We took. To get here.

Some days. I only. Hear the rain. In my head. As if it starts. There and then. Goes out. Into the world. That without it. Would fall silent. And silence. We would. Hear attend. All until. One perfect. Drop collapses. Into the vale. Of our touching. Hands that began. Apart but moved. Together on the balustrade. As we watched. The sea. And over there. Behind clouds. That began. Together but moved. Apart the sun.

During the collapse. We'll hear. The sounds. Of every world. Mine and yours. The world. Of mammals. The world. Of birds. The world. Of wind and rain. Feel. Your hand. Move away. And there again. The silence. We'll search. Your favorite book. For a tree. To wait. Under. There are many. On the path. To your home. Or my home. Or neither. We'll lean. Over the pages. So they don't. Get wet. And choose. One. We haven't. Waited. Under before.

And see. There is one. In a garden. Through a garden. Gate. And decide. We'll wait. There. If the rain. Continues. But if it. Stops. We'll go. Our separate. Ways. And another. Day. Share. The stories. Of our lifetime. Perspectives. But if not. Want to. The woman is. Still there. Talking to you. Sometimes. She stands. Near me. And whispers. What she's. Saying. I only. Hear. The words. But not. Her breathing. In between.

xliii

You're hiding. Something. In your pocket. That needs. Special holding. A beautiful. Object. Given. To you. By someone. You love. At the kitchen. Table. You'll show me. In the palm. Of your hand. And move. It into. The light. Near the window. I'll watch. The reflection. Of your face. From the darkness. A bird will. Fly. Into the glass. We'll see it. On the ground. Beneath the window. Pane. And with one eye. It will see. Us too. And fly away. Before it heals.

It's not. A dream. We'll turn. The kitchen table. Upside down. And take it. To the air. Hold on. To the table legs. And follow. The bird between. The clouds. It knows. Where to go. You can sit. And I can. Stand. The wind. Will blow. Your hair. You'll tell me. To watch out. For the electrical. Wires. And the water. Towers. The airplanes. The migration. Of southern flying. Birds. And if. We have travelled. Far enough. Together. The moon. The stars. And the sun.

And I'll stand. Perfectly still. Like a captain. On a swaying. Ship to keep. My balance. And if there's. Rain. You won't. Notice. I'll cover. Your head. With a tree. Branch of leaves. I'll take. With me. From the world. Below. We can. Have our life. Up here too. I wonder. If I will. Put. My arms. By my side. Or reach out. To you. So you'll know. Not to tell. Me to watch. Out for anything. Again. I feel. When I look. At you. Who could not. Look at you. And fall. In love.

And above. The dome. From where. The starlings flew. I'll see. The sun. As the clouds. Dissolve. It seems. The rain. Is stopping. Over there. And will. Stop. Here too. But how. Soon. Or if. At all. I can't know. Will I follow. You. Or come back. To wait. Another day. When it rains. To find. You again. As I might. Find my place. In a book. Being read. Out loud. By someone. Else.

I'll pretend. To turn. The pages. To look. Ahead. Turn. Them back. And use. My powers. Of deduction. To find. The words. Being spoken. So that. What I see. And what. Is said. Is in harmony. Until. The end. As the sun. Like an orb. Of fire. Descends. And night. Comes when. Everyone. Has gone. And the stage. And all. The seats. Beneath. The (starry) sky. Are empty. I'll be. The last. To leave. Or lie. Across two chairs. And fall. Asleep.

xlviii

And dream. Of myself. Watching. You. Sleep across. Two chairs. Beneath. The sky. Like me. Though in. My dream. I am awake. And there. Are no stars. Maybe. All the stars. Were used. To fashion. You. Barely breathing. So that you're. Beautiful. And the person. Reading. Out loud. Is gone. No one. Thinks. Of the words. He said. But if. They followed. In the book. He wrote called. Bend Human. Willing. They can. Remember them. *This is my dream. And in my dream. You're dreaming too.*

xlix

I don't know. What to do. If the rain. Stops. I watch. The clouds. Vanish. Across the city. Scape see. The sun. And blue. Sky umbrellas. Closing. One by. One along. The way leading. To the stranger. Walking past. You wearing. A pretty. Summer dress. She'll close. Her umbrella. And carry it. Beneath her arm. You'll look. Up. To the sky. Before leaving.

1

We're strangers too. In a photograph. Taken. By a tourist. Shown to family. And friends. Though someone. Will notice. Us on. Either end framing. The couple. In the foreground. Smiling beneath. A black umbrella. And those two. Back there. A little. Blurry but clear. Enough to see. Who knows. Who they are. Or what. They're thinking. The photograph. Would look. Better without. Them everyone agrees.

li

But there. Is one. Perhaps taken. By a child. Of his mother. And father. Where the angle. Makes it look. Like you're standing. Right in front. Of me. Your hand. Above. Your shoulder. Touching. My face. Someone. Might complain. He or she. Was never. Touched that way. Though you'd. Only lifted. Your hand. To check. For rain. And someone else. Seeing the same. Photograph. In many years. Might look. Past the smiling. Couple and wonder. If those two. Back there. Are still. Together.

lii

I remember. On my way. To school. A path. To the woods. Where the grass. Looked trampled. On though. I had never. Seen anyone. Go that way. I've walked. Past there since. But never through. It still. Looks the same. It seems. The grass. Never died. But also. Never grew. Nothing was. Planted. An unmapped. Piece of land. No wars. Were ever. Fought for. I think. I'll take you. There after. The rain.

liii

On a day. Sunshine. Spreads over. The trees. Like a fan. Unfolding. No one. Would see. Us it would. Be too bright. As we walked. Through the open. Space and faded. Into the light. Holding hands. And then into. The woods. On the other. Side we could. Turn back. If we got. Scared. Or quietly be. Brave—try. Though no one. Would know. Or cared. If we. Ran away maybe. They'd think. We were running. From being happy.

Like we did. During recess. Or on. The last day. Of school. When we. Weren't standing. Beneath. Two trees. Like we're standing. Now. And the deluge. Filtered. By the leaves. Two. Drops of rain. Slipping. From leaf. To leaf. Falling. On me. And on you. I feel. It on my. Skin beneath. My eye. Someone peeking. From beneath. Her umbrella. As she walked. By might. See. You there inside. Like a scene. From a movie. Playing. In a tear. Drop. Of rain.

In school. We might. Have been. Friends. Who later. Drifted apart. And remembered. Each other. Only as a feeling. During a certain. Season. A girl. I played with. And may. Have loved. In that way. Lost. Beneath time. Like a hill. Of leaves. My memory. Like an aimless. Breeze. Unsettles. To find. I hope. You're still. Around. Maybe sitting. Next to me. On the bus. Or standing. Over there. Beneath the tree.

Or in. The elevator. Where we lean. Against the elevator. Walls. On either side. As people. Shuffle in. And out. Replaced by. Others. The bell rings. For each floor. And with. Each ring. I hope for. Something more. For you. And me. Small hopes. Nothing big. A softer pillow. To lay your. Head on. As you sleep. And in. The morning. Wake to hear. The curtain. Opening. Like a bead. On an abacus. That counts. Another day. Of you. And me. Together.

And not losing. It the thing. It seems. So many. Have lost. As they sit. On busses. Or stand. Beneath trees. Or lean against. Elevator walls. As people. Are replaced. These spaces. Are small. But still. Too big. Become too filled. We need. A smaller space. In which only. We can fit. Something no larger. Than a grave. From where. We can watch. Some. Of the world. Enough. At least. The different. Kinds of clouds. Sometimes the sun. If it passes. By and at night. The moon. If we're lucky. And the stars.

I see. Their light. Shining. On your fingers. Pretending. To play. The piano. On your kitchen. Table. The way. You practiced. On your desk. At school. I imagined. The black. And white keys. With you before. The last bell. Rang and you. Gathered your books. To hurry. To a nearby. House. Where my mother. Taught you. How to play. We never. Walked there. Together. I always waited. And walked. After you.

lix

I would see. You sitting. At the piano. And pass. By within inches. To see. Your back. And neck. You'd put your. Hair up. When you. Were there. Something you never. Did and no. One ever saw. At school. My mother. Said you. Didn't play. Very well. Didn't practice. Enough but from. My room I. Liked hearing. How you stopped. And started. And the silence. In between.

The next day. I'd see you. As if. You were standing. Beneath a tree. Across the way. Waiting for. A friend. A kiss. On the cheek. A smile. A hand. On the lower. Back and tea. A few minutes. Later at a café. I sit. There and think. I can only. Be the person. I want. To be when. I'm (writing). In those moments. That bring you. Here to me.

Another letter. I enclose. In an unaddressed. Envelope. About an examination. Of the tree. You stood under. In which. I find. A black hole. An escaping. Universe. And in it. A single. Star. A sun. Around which. You. My unexplored. Planet revolve. I stand. Where you stood. And imagine. How you. Might have. Seen the world. And in. The world me.

The trees. Aren't just. Happy. They're also sad. And this bright. Sky. Isn't just. Bright. It's also dark. And on. A bicycle. At night. It feels. No one. Is real. But me. I only. Hear the wind. And the piece. Of road. That comes. Quickly and just. As quickly. Goes under. My front. Wheel everything. Behind me. Is silence. And darkness. If I turn. To see. What's left. Back. There I'll crash. And I do.

You'll hear. The wreck. And through. Your apartment window. See. The wreckage. You won't. Recognize me. As I lift. The bicycle. To leave. You'll look up. To the sky. And think under. All of that. No one. Else but you. Is real. And hear just. The lamp click. When you. Turn the light. Switch. I'll see. The light go. Off in my. Periphery. But won't. Turn to look. I'll keep riding. Away.

But I didn't. Ride that day. I walked. And when. The rain came. I stopped. Under the tree. Across from you. While around us. People. With umbrellas moved. Like blood. Cells along. Narrow arteries. And the other. Paths leading. To a heart. Far from. Here or. Maybe right here. Between us. We people. Who wait. Under trees. After the invention. Of umbrellas.

We can leave. Small objects. By the roots. To let. People know. We were there. They'd have. To endure. The weather. Like we did. The wind. And the cold. But our story. Would be told. By a hair. Brush or. A leather glove. And on the tree. Above a black. Bird lingers. To steal. One of them. Away. So the other. Would look. Misplaced. Instead of placed.

Then at night. When the streets. Were empty. Of people. And the moon. Was bright. The breeze. From a passing. Truck the engine. Heard for half. A mile. Just might give. The fingers. Of the glove. The impression. Of life. And unsettle. A strand of. The woman's hair. Caught. In the bristles. Of the brush. That come morning. A butterfly. Would mistake. For rows. Of small flowers.

Something magical. You leaned. Against the tree. Its trunk. And limbs. The shape. Of a hand. Around you. Ready to close. Should something. Come your. Way. A shield against. The whims. Of everyday. Life and me. Or was it. Your way. Of saying. Do something. Don't wait. Until the rain. Stops. And the light. Dims and our. Time here. Together ends.

lxviii

A time. In which. The second. Hand pauses. Between this. Second and the next. And with it. All forms. Of motion. And sound. It's possible. Our eyes met. But how quickly. The chance. Is lost. To take. Another way. The rain stops. The wind blows. And the small. White flowers. Wet and burdened. Drop from. Their pedicels. Onto the concrete. Below.

In a moment. You'd be gone. And I wouldn't. See which. Way you'd go. I'd search. All around. But even with. The sun. Shining on. The whole world. You could. Still hide. In the darkness. Up there. And watch me. Through the leaves. As I scratch. The rough. Bark with. A sharp rock. The only. Thing I know. So that years. From now. If the tree. Is still standing. I'll remember. The day. I caught you. When you fell. And carried you. From here.

I know if. Something happened to. You I'd never. Stand under. A tree. Again to grow. Old and die. Together. Under the sun. Or in. The rain. But if not. I'll remember you. As a faint. Feeling like. The degraded. DNA of those. Who got away. Kept safely. Somewhere on. The other side. Of a closed. Door a face. I know. Is there. But will never. Be revealed. Unless the future. Keeps its. Promise to make. All things possible.

It's surprising. How strength returns. After so many. Years where did. It go and from. Where will it. Return. Why didn't it. Take me too. Leaving me. Instead under. A tree. My body. A camouflet. Exposed to you. Too weak. For everyday human. Movements and gestures. I can. Mimic strength. Under here. While it rains. Held up. By the tree. Limbs above. Me like. The hands. Of a puppeteer. And I. The puppet.

I see. The sun. Two clouds parting. Like the eye. Of the world. Opening after. A deep sleep. A sleepy day. In the rain. Now time. To be awake. Maybe it's dreaming. About us. We people. Who wait. Under trees. After the invention. Of umbrellas. But there's too. Much to see. And doesn't see. We're real. Close it again. World sleep. So we can. Stay here. A little while. Longer.

Where is. This home. Of ours. As we leave. Me in front. Leading you. Across puddles. Not yet. Evaporated. By the sun. Then arriving. Feel the breeze. The curtain. Reaching into. Our small room. Because we. Had left. The window. Open I'll. Close it. Pause to gaze. At everything. We left. Behind and see. Your reflection. In the glass. Like a ghost. Among the trees.

lxxiv

People like. Their symmetries. They say we're. Alone on both. Ends though we. Never come. Into the. World alone. It's possible. We'll leave. That way. But until then. We hope. Our time. Together will. Be long. Our sadness contained. Our happiness unfenced. And everything. We choose. To have. Or choose. To do. Hold the possibility. Of beauty. And love.

Together enfolded. In the curtain. Someone might. Look up and. Seeing us. In the window. For a moment. Think they see. A painting. Hung on. The faded brick. But looking. Again see. That we're gone. And maybe. Later that day. Remember what. They saw. A memory. They'll keep. To themselves. Forever. Because in. The end. Really. What was there. To tell.

The sun. Goes down. Behind tall buildings. In the distance. Replaced by. Street lamps. All around. There is one. Between our. Two trees. An orange glow. In which I see. Drops of rain. Falling frantic. Chased down from. Drifting clouds. Something's coming. From behind. Them more sinister. Than night. Even the stars. That shined. So brightly. Yesterday are overcome. And the grey. Sky so many. Had lamented. Turns black.

This is. Where we can. Do all we. Were too afraid. To do the day. Is gone and all. The eyes. Of night are closed. This darkness. Is not death. Is not waking. In the morning. And thinking. This could be. The last morning. I wake up. Beside you. Or seeing. You walk by. An opened door. Beautiful and adored. Thinking. This could be. The last time. I see you. How is it. Good for a human. To think. This way before. The end. And yet. We think. This way. Because we. Are afraid.

It's still. Raining and someone. Else has come. For you. With her umbrella. Time for me. To leave. But I will remember. This day. I hope. You will. Remember. This day too. All the street. Noises have returned. The engines. Of cars. The footfalls. Of passersby. You will go. Your way. And I will. Go mine. And the space. Beneath our two. Trees will be. Empty except for. A searching breeze.

epilogue

one day they'll build a bench across from where
we stood so people can sit when they're waiting
for the bus and over time the bench will age from
weather its bolts rusted its wood stripped of stain
and our two trees cut to make way for some
artificial thing no one will know they once stood
there i'll go that way sometimes and then less so
only showing up like someone might drive
through an old neighborhood after many years
i'll never have the chance to sit on the bench and
gaze at what was once there always traveling in
something that can't stop passing through a place
along the way to somewhere else

Running isn't...
ART museum...
painting on...
woman from...
can't remem...
and I lost tr...
think I had be...
hours. The r...
security guards chasing me
but I ran track in high school

It was AS I was looking at
myself running and running
at the same time, with the
guards chasing me from my
perspective and from their
perspective... from my
... looked like
they were returning to
me... but... their
p...

I s...
mo...
se...
wh...
th...
wa...
the special exhibitions area
that A guard asked me to
stop, and when I didn't stop,
took chase. I heard him

we
can
make
it
if
we
run

18th century where it was
slowed by the BEAUTIFUL
Madame Le Fèvre de
...
...ge I considered to
...ardly hidden by a
peony and little
peony stem (oh

I paused for the f...
moments in the 1...
to take in the A...
Harbor before I...
WOMAN and gi...
horseback (that's...
was running)...
curious "Sab...
Swedenborgh who looked as if
she wanted to follow me